Pinklejinx

by

Tish Dahlby

Pictures by

Kory Fluckiger

Pinklejinx Press

ISBN 978-0-9857678-3-9 (hardcover)
Second Edition

Manufactured in China
ShenZhen Wei Mei Printing Co., LTD

For more information on Pinklejinx, products and characters visit
Pinklejinx at: www.pinklejinx.com

pinklejinx ®

To my husband, Gregg, and daughters, Rachel, Hannah, Ellen and Lena, thank you for bringing **joy** into my life. –T.D.

To Dick, thank you for believing. –T.D.

To Roma, *my* joy. –K.F.

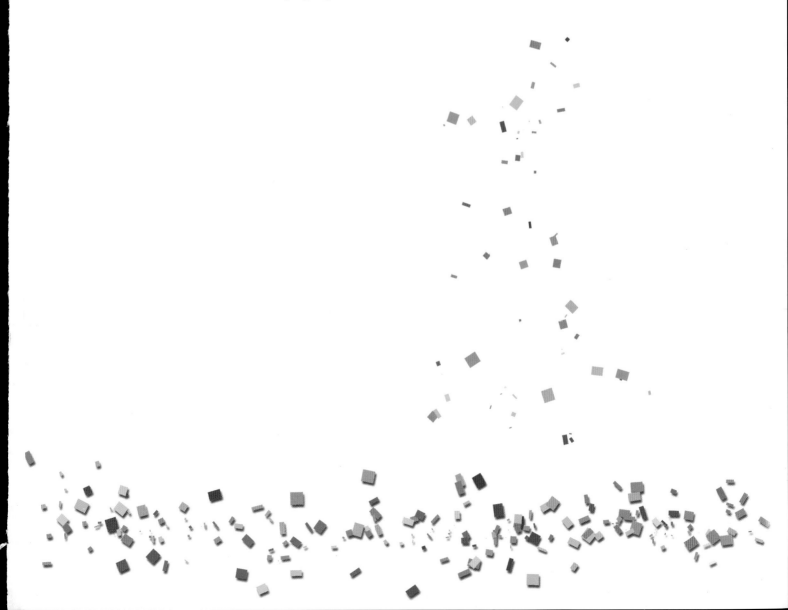

Jubilee is a place like no other. Here, the mountains are giant party hats sprinkled with confetti snowflakes, and jumbo birthday candles light the streets.

Mr Poppers

TOYS

Miss Fedora

Hat Shop

Bakery

But the most spectacular sight
of all is the bakery, the home of
the baker and his daughter, Joy.

Joy loves birthdays more than anything, so it is perfect that she lives in Jubilee. Every morning, Joy and her dog, Cupcake, awaken to the sound of the alarm clock singing *Happy Birthday*.

Leaping out of bed, Joy places her baker's hat on her head. Eyes tightly shut, she makes her daily wish.

"I want to be a birthday fairy and bring *joy* to everyone, everywhere on their birthday!"

With a big puff, Joy blows out her imaginary birthday candles.

"Fiddlesticks! My wish didn't come true. Fairy
or not, I want to make birthdays special... but how?"
Her father's bubbly voice rises from the bakery.
"Joy, my joy, awake. The time has come to bake!"

Joy slides into her father's arms. The two bakers laugh, eager to start their day.

"How many cakes will we bake today, Daddy?"

Glancing at the birthday calendar, Joy's father counts aloud, "One, two, three cakes: Miss Petunia from the flower shop, Mr. Reed the librarian, and Sally who will be turning six!"

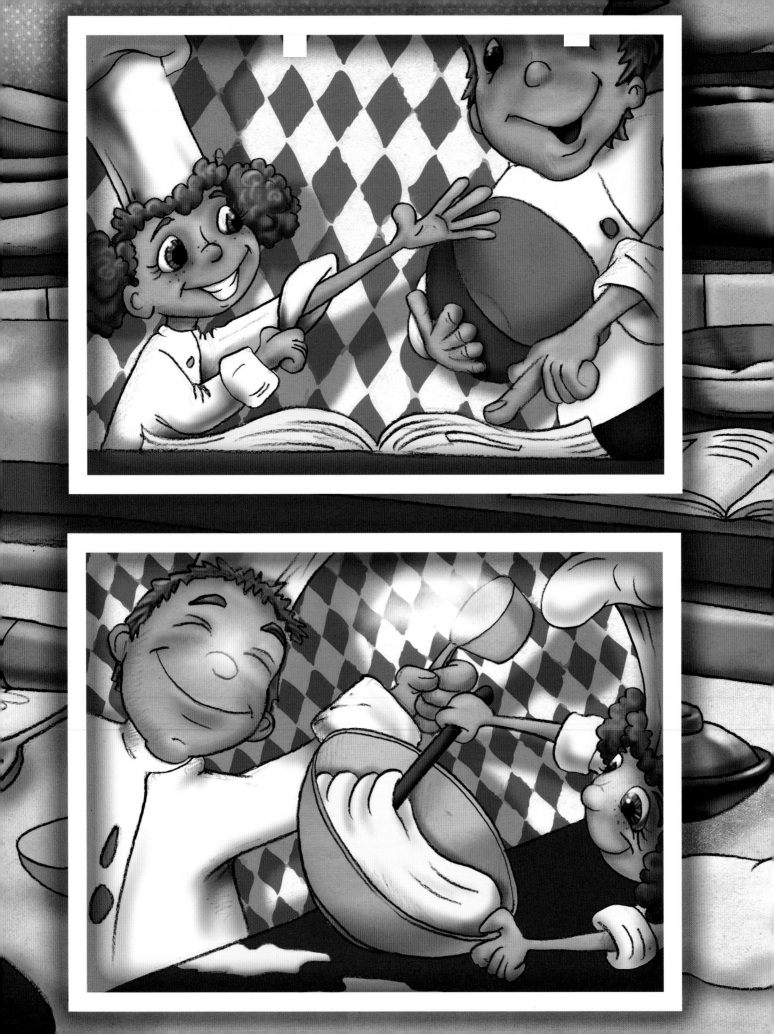

Joy puts on her apron and rolls up her sleeves. The two bakers open the recipe book and work side by side, carefully gathering, measuring, and mixing the ingredients.

Joy pours the batter into the pans, and her father places them in the oven and sets the timer.

"Mmmmmm," says Joy, as the sweet aroma fills the air.

While the cakes cool, Joy frolics through the village, gathering birthday treasures for each celebration. At the party store, Mr. Popper helps her choose the perfect balloons and ribbons. Together they blow up balloons until they are too dizzy to stand.

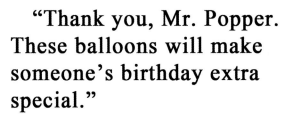

"Thank you, Mr. Popper. These balloons will make someone's birthday extra special."

Giggling at the thought of floating away, Joy walks to Miss Fedora's hat shop. "Oh, *this* must be how it feels to be a *real* birthday fairy," she tells Cupcake.

"Bonjour, Mademoiselle Joy!" Miss Fedora greets her. "Ready to make festive party hats?"

"Ta-da!" cries Joy, as she models her creation.

"A birthday crown," Miss Fedora gushes. "How exquisite!"

Feeling very proud, Joy thinks to herself, "Yes, this is how a *real* birthday fairy must feel."

All morning, Joy and Cupcake add to their collection of goodies.

"What a good birthday fairy I would make," says Joy.

"Woof, woof!" Cupcake agrees.

Back at the bakery, it is time to decorate the birthday cakes.

Delicious frosting oozes from the pastry bags as the baker and his daughter pipe colorful confections onto the cakes. Counting out the candles, Joy carefully sets each one in its place.

"Now for the final touch," cheers Joy.

Her father reaches for the special jar marked "Pinklejinx." He shakes the glittery concoction onto each cake, reciting:

"A sprinkle of Pinklejinx on a cake baked for you.
May the wish that you hold in your heart now come true."

Every night, Joy helps her father pack up the cakes and birthday kits. She smiles as her father's wings unfurl. Joy kisses her father, the Birthday Fairy, goodbye as he sets off to decorate homes for early morning celebrations.

"It feels very good to make people happy,"
Joy thinks, "especially on their birthdays."

And each night, Joy falls asleep dreaming of one day becoming a *real* birthday fairy.

One exceptional morning, Joy awakens to the familiar tune of *Happy Birthday*. But this time it is not coming from her alarm clock.

She races downstairs…

...and is greeted by all the villagers of Jubilee.

At the table, a place of honor is set just for her.
"A birthday plate and cup," Joy giggles. "Why
even my fork and spoon look like candles!"
Joy munches on her scrumptious birthday breakfast.
Never has she felt more special.

Seeing her birthday cake, Joy claps. "Ooooh, it's magnificent but…"

The elder baker winks knowingly. And for the first time ever, he offers his daughter the jar of Pinklejinx.

Joy already knows her wish. Squeezing her eyes shut, she whispers, "I want to be a birthday fairy and bring *joy* to everyone, everywhere on their birthday."

Shaking the glistening glitter on her cake, Joy recites:
"A sprinkle of Pinklejinx on a cake baked for ME.
May the wish that I hold in my heart come to BE!"

This time Joy is not dreaming.
Her cake and the candles are very real.

"Hooray!" Joy shouts. Her wish has finally come true!

After a day of celebration, Joy scoops up Cupcake.

"It's time for bed. Tomorrow will come soon enough. I have many cakes to bake and homes to decorate in Jubilee and all around the world. Now I know exactly how it feels to be a *real* birthday fairy!"

Each night, Joy, the Birthday Fairy, packs up special boxes with birthday dishes, decorations, and of course, a jar of Pinklejinx—the magical birthday glitter filled with love and good wishes.

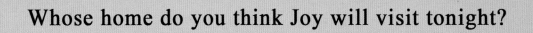

Whose home do you think Joy will visit tonight?